What's Up in the Attic?

SESAME STREET

CTW

By Liza Alexander
Illustrated by Tom Cooke

Featuring Jim Henson's Ses~ ~ppets

A Sesame Street/Golden Press Book

Published by Western Publishing Company, Inc., in conjunction with Children's Television Workshop.

It was a drizzly gray day on Sesame Street. Ernie listened to the dreary sound of the rain against the window. "There's nothing to do!" he groaned.

"Cheer up, Ern!" said Bert. "How about a game of Duckie Land? It used to be our favorite! Come on! Let's go up to the attic and find it!"

Bert gave Ernie a flashlight, and they climbed up the steep stairs to the attic door.

"Ho, hum," sighed Ernie. From the window at the top of the landing he watched the swollen rain clouds scuttle across the sky.

The windows let some light into the gloomy attic. Bert found a couple of old-fashioned lamps and turned them on.

Ernie shined his flashlight around the musty attic. "Wow!" he said, cheering up. "There's lots of great junk up here! Where's Oscar when we need him? Hee, hee!"

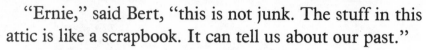

"Ernie," said Bert, "this is not junk. The stuff in this attic is like a scrapbook. It can tell us about our past."

Ernie knelt down beside a big old trunk. "Look at this, Bert. It's Great-Aunt Ernestine's trunk. It's been everywhere! Here's a sticker of the Eiffel Tower. That's in Paris, France. And here's a sticker showing the Golden Gate Bridge. That means it's from San Francisco."

"Wouldn't you like to travel and see the world when you grow up?" Bert asked Ernie. "*I* would."

Bert pulled a fringed jacket out of the trunk. "This trunk is full of family things. This frontier jacket belonged to my grandfather's grandfather, old Mountain Mike. They say he once wrestled a bear to the ground with his bare hands. He had a coonskin cap, too! Let's look for it!"

"Okay, Bert," said Ernie. "A coonskin cap would be
pretty neat. We could use it to play cowboy."

"And it would remind us of the old days," said Bert.
"I'd look pretty sharp in a coonskin cap. Yessirree! Now,
where is it?"

Ernie climbed up on a chair to poke around on top of a
wardrobe. Lots of boxes were up there.

Bert dug down deeper into the trunk. "Oh, look what I found, Ernie!" cried Bert. "Uncle Bart's antique paper-clip collection."

"Uh, what's an antique, old buddy?" asked Ernie.

"It's something very old. Some antiques are special because they are different from what we use today, and some are special because they belonged to someone important. Good old Uncle Bart! He gave me my very first paper clip."

Ernie and Bert forgot all about looking for Duckie Land. They even forgot about the rain. But Bert did not forget about the coonskin cap. "It's got to be here somewhere!" said Bert.

Searching in a far corner, Ernie brushed aside some cobwebs and found his old tricycle. It was much too tiny for him now.

"My, how I've grown!" said Ernie, his
knees all scrunched up as he pedaled his
trike. "Let's see how fast this baby can go!"

"Stop it, Ernie!" yelled Bert as Ernie crashed around the attic at high speed. He knocked past the wardrobe, and some of the hatboxes tumbled to the floor.

Ernie screeched to a halt in front of a dressmaker's dummy. Bert wiped his brow. "Phew!" he said.

Then Bert discovered an old-fashioned record player called a Victrola. He put a record on it and cranked it up to make it go.

Nearby, Ernie found a fancy black jacket and a top hat, and he put them on. "May I have this dance?" he asked the dummy. They waltzed around and around to the Victrola's tinny music as Bert snapped his fingers to the beat.

"Look," said Bert. "It's Dandy the Rocking Horse. Remember what fun we had riding her when we were little?"

Bert put on Mountain Mike's jacket. He jumped into Dandy's saddle and began to sing, "Home, home on the range...where the deer and the antelope play...

"Shucks," said Bert. "I sure wish I had that coonskin cap."

Ernie slung an old brown rug over his shoulders and lumbered up behind Bert. "Grrrrrrrr," he said. "I am a bear. Dare you to wrestle me to the ground like old Mountain Mike!"

"Don't be ridiculous," said Bert as he swung down off Dandy. "We've got to find that coonskin cap!"

Then Bert found something interesting. "Oh, my goodness! Here is one of Bernice's baby pigeon feathers. I forgot I saved it. And here is her baby picture. Wasn't she an adorable chick?"

"All right! Look at this!" said Ernie. "My old
marbles." He gathered the marbles and looked around
for something to put them in.

Then Ernie spotted a furry tail amid the boxes. It was
attached to Mountain Mike's coonskin cap!

"Bert will be so happy!" Ernie said to himself as he
tossed the marbles into the cap.

Bert was so busy searching that he didn't notice what Ernie was doing.

"The coonskin cap isn't here anymore," he said with a sigh, taking a last look around the attic. "Let's go back downstairs. The sun is coming out anyway."

Ernie balanced all his family treasures in the tricycle basket and rode over to Bert. Ernie plopped the cap on his head, and the marbles from the hat clattered all over the floor.

"Ernie!" said Bert. "You've lost your... Hey, you found it! Mountain Mike's coonskin cap!"

"Sure, Bert. Just for you!" said Ernie, and he gave Bert the cap.

"Ernie, what are you planning to do with all this junk?" asked Bert.

"This stuff is just what our place needs," said Ernie. "A dressmaker's dummy, a tiny tricycle, a top hat, and a fuzzy brown rug. Help me carry a few little things, Bert!"

So they carried all their attic discoveries down the stairs.

"This afternoon up in the attic was fun," said Ernie to Bert. "I'm glad I thought of it."